Ju
F
R73   Rosman, Steven M.
            Deena the damselfly.

Ju
F
R73   Rosman, Steven M.
            Deena the damselfly.

Temple Israel Library
Minneapolis, Minn.

———

Please sign your full name on the above card.

Return books promptly to the Library or Temple Office.

Fines will be charged for overdue books or for damage or loss of same.

DEENA THE DAMSELFLY

DEENA THE DAMSELFLY

Steven M. Rosman
Illustrated by Giora Carmi

UAHC Press
New York, New York

To my wife, Bari,
who gives me the inspiration and the support I need to
write my stories

To my daughter, Mikki,
for whom I write them and tell them

I love you both

Library of Congress Cataloging-in-Publication Data

Rosman, Steven M.
    Deena the damselfly/Steven M. Rosman; illustrated
by Giora Carmi.
        p. cm.
    Summary: Deena, a damselfly nymph, vows to solve
the mystery of why the older nymphs are disappearing
when they reach maturity, but she is not prepared for
her own startling transformation.
    ISBN 0-8074-0477-2 (hardcover: acid-free paper):
$10.95
    [1. Damselflies—Fiction.] I. Karmi, Giyora, ill. II. Title.
PZ7.R71954De 1992   91-43472
[E]—dc20   CIP
                                                  AC

This book is printed on acid-free paper
Copyright © 1992 by Steven M. Rosman
Manufactured in the United States of America
10 9 8 7 6 5 4 3 2 1

ACKNOWLEDGMENTS

The completion of this project is due to the talented contributions of many people. Were it not for the deft and artistic editing of Aron Hirt-Manheimer, let alone for his constant encouragement and enduring support, there would be no tale. Were it not for the generous and selfless efforts of my secretary and "right hand," Kathy Thomson, there would be no text to edit. Were it not for the help and entomological "know-how" of Juanita Hall and Joe Smith at the National Museum of Natural History in Washington, D.C., and Dr. Sid Dunkle at the International Odonata Research Institute in Gainesville, Florida, there would have been no nymphs or damselflies to write about.

I am truly fortunate to have received the skillful and caring help from all who are mentioned above. Their combined contributions, along with the evocative and fantastic illustrations of the renowned Giora Carmi, gave life to a tale I am delighted to share.

Have you ever seen a nymph?
Come visit the pond. There they
are, crawling among the blades
of sweet-smelling grass! Long
and slippery, they dart across
the water.

Nymphs love the warm comfort
of their pond. When it is sunny,
they soak up the heat, then cool
themselves in the damp sand.
When it rains, they dive under
the water and listen to the
raindrops tapping the pond's
surface like a drum.

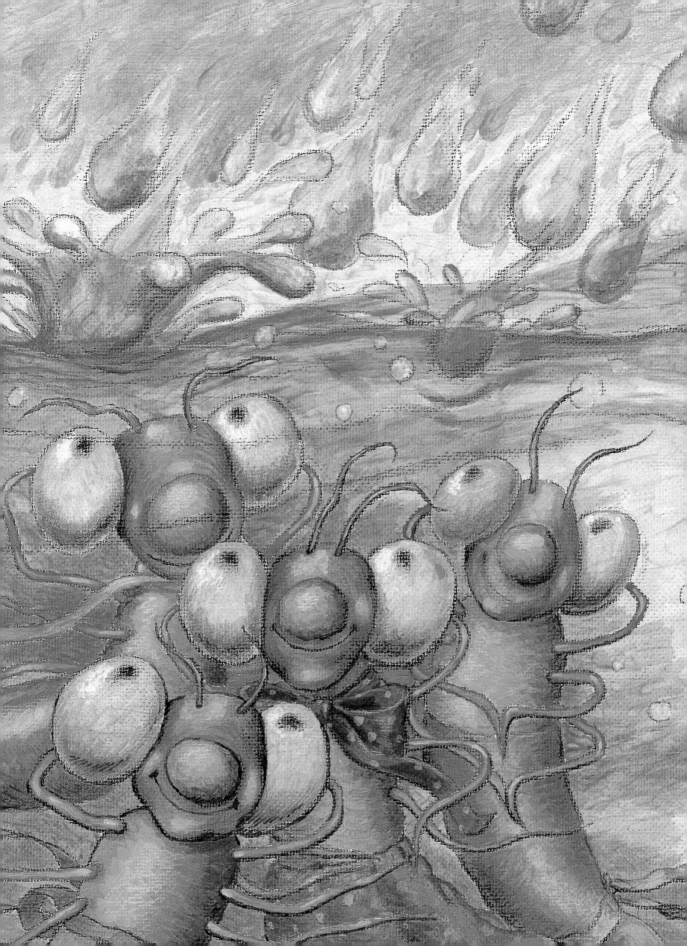

So, you see, nymphs are very
happy creatures. There is,
however, one troubling mystery
that has never been solved:
When nymphs reach a certain
age, they disappear. One day
they are playing in the water
like everyone else, and the next
day they are gone, without
telling anyone they're going
away.

One young nymph named Deena was curious about all this. She promised that, when she got older and disappeared, she would come back to the pond and tell her friends where she had gone.

Deena called all her friends together and gave them her promise. Then she rose up as straight as she could and flapped her gills in the damp sand three times. That is how nymphs make promises. Her friends bounced with joy. Finally someone was going to solve the mystery.

Time passed. Deena and her friends continued to play in their pond. Older nymphs disappeared, and still no one knew where they went.

One day, Deena felt very strange. She crawled to the water's edge and slowly climbed to the top of a large twig. She did not know why she was climbing, only that she had to. When she reached the top of the twig, a strange feeling shook her body. She felt different from before.

Then a miracle occurred.

Deena began to rise in the air. She was flying. She looked to her sides and saw beautiful wings attached to her body. Flying was easy and fun, like playing in the damp sand by the pond.

Far below she could see the clouds and the blue sky reflected by the water's surface. Flying lower, Deena saw a strange creature with a shiny dark body and rainbow-colored wings.

"Who is that beautiful creature?" she asked herself, looking around. "I don't see anyone. The only one flying above the pond is me. Me! Me! It can't be!"

But it was. Deena the nymph
had become Deena the
damselfly. She no longer looked
like a nymph, neither did she
sound like one. Her voice was
different.

Remembering her promise,
Deena flew to the spot where
her nymph friends were playing.
No one recognized her, and, no
matter how loud she screamed,
no one answered.

"It's me, it's me! Deena! Can't
you hear me? I have come back
to keep my promise. I know
where all our friends
disappeared to and what
happened to them. Can't
anyone hear me?" No one heard
her. Finally, Deena flew away to
join her new friends.

Back at the pond, Deena's nymph friends wondered what had happened to her and if she would keep her promise.

Deena did not return to the pond. "What's the point. They do not know who I am."

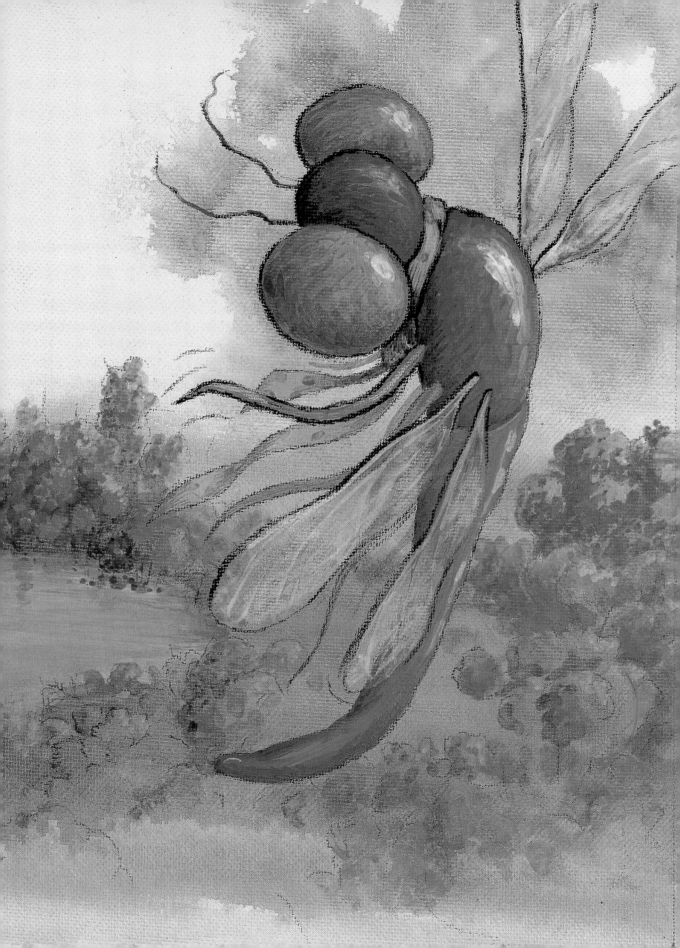

Deena now spent her time playing with her damselfly friends. But she never forgot her old friends by the pond. She knew that someday they too would become damselflies just like her. That thought made her smile.